EGMONT

We bring stories to life

This edition published in Great Britain 2009 by Dean,
an imprint of Egmont UK Limited
239 Kensington High Street, London W8 6SA
All Rights Reserved

Thomas the Tank Engine & Friends™

HiT entertainment

ISBN 978 0 6035 6386 7
1 3 5 7 9 10 8 6 4 2
Printed and bound in Singapore

THOMAS
and the Hurricane

The Rev. W. Awdry
Illustrated by Robin Davies

A howling gale was blowing across the Island of Sodor. None of the engines got much sleep that night.
"Brrr!" shivered Thomas as he struggled to wake up in the morning. The wind was cold as well as strong – it blew leaves and litter into the Shed.

There weren't many passengers that morning.
They all wanted to stay indoors and Thomas didn't
blame them. "Lucky things," he said to himself.

But when Thomas reached the station by the river, he was astonished to see footballers playing in the nearby field. One team was wearing red shirts, while the other was in blue.

"It's part of the Knockout Competition," explained the Fireman. "At the end of the season, the winners will get a silver cup."

The trees between the field and the railway waved wildly
in the wind.
"Sooner them than me," Thomas muttered to himself.
"They'll all get knocked out if they're not careful!"

James was waiting at the junction. He didn't mind the wind, he said, and was even boasting about it. "My train was right on time," he announced proudly. "A little bit of wind can't stop me."

Just then the wind blew so hard that the station roof shook . . .
and so did something else.
"Just look at that signal!" exclaimed Thomas.

"Signal – what signal?" James asked. Suddenly, the signal gantry wasn't there any more. The gale had blown it down.

"Help!" said Thomas in alarm, as two more signal posts broke and crashed to the ground. "Let's get away from here."

The Fireman hurried to the signal-box to find out what they should do.
"We can't move without any signals," explained the Driver.
"How will we know if it's safe?"

"Well, it's not safe here either," snorted James. "That's no wind, it's a hurricane!"

The Drivers laughed, but they did move the engines along the platform as far as they dared.

It was lucky that they did, because two minutes later the wind lifted the platform canopy clean off its framework and dropped it, to shatter on the platform below.

No one was hurt as the canopy crashed down, but Annie and Clarabel were very frightened, and some splinters of wood had scratched Clarabel's paint.

At last a man with flags came and signalled the two trains away.
James forgot his boasting and was only too glad to get going.
Thomas followed a safe distance behind.

Thomas had the wind behind him now, and by the time he reached the curve near the football ground he was steaming along well. They were halfway round the bend when suddenly there was a jerk, and the Guard's emergency brake went on hard.

"Ooooooooer," groaned Thomas. "What's the matter now?"
He soon found out. Lying across the line in front of him were several enormous fallen trees. Thomas' brakes bit hard and he stopped just in time.

The Driver looked back. Running towards them were three footballers followed by the Guard who was waving his flag and blowing his whistle.

"So that's how the Guard knew when to brake," said Thomas.
"Thank goodness you stopped," panted the footballers when they
arrived. "We thought we were too late."
"It was a near thing," said the Driver. "Thank you for warning us."

Later that day, Terence the Tractor came and dragged the trees off the line. Trevor was busy in the field using his circular saw to cut up the wood while Toby and Percy worked hard all day taking the logs away.

Evening came, and at last the line was clear.
Thomas and Annie and Clarabel could go home.

A week later there was a party at the riverside station.
The Fat Controller gave all the footballers a silver cup as a
thank-you for saving the train. "You may not have won the
tournament," he laughed, "but you certainly beat that hurricane!"